DISCARD

P9-DUI-534

Winston & George

www.enchantedlionbooks.com

This book has been set in Bembo, an old-style humanist serif typeface originally cut by Francesco Griffo
in 1495 and revived by Stanley Morison in 1929.

First American edition published in 2014 by Enchanted Lion Books, 351 Van Brunt Street, Brooklyn, NY 11231
Copyright © 2014 Enchanted Lion Books
Text copyright © 2014 by John Miller
Illustrations copyright © 2014 by the family of Giuliano Cucco
Crocodile photo copyright © StuPorts/Photos.com
Crocodile bird photo copyright © 2013 by Steven Garvie
All rights reserved under International and Pan-American Copyright Conventions. A CIP record is on file with the Library of Congress
ISBN: 978-1-59270-145-2. Printed and bound in November 2013 by South China Printing Company
Design and layout by Lawrence Kim

Winston & George

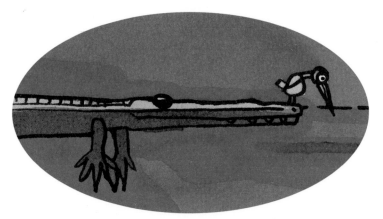

Story by
John Miller

Illustrations by
Giuliano Cucco

ENCHANTED LION BOOKS
NEW YORK

Along a sleepy river deep in the jungle, there once lived a very, very patient crocodile called Winston. Now this crocodile and a crocodile bird named George were especially good friends, and they spent each day together out on the river fishing.

George would perch on the very tip of Winston's snout, looking into the water for fish, and the moment he spied one, he would shout "DIVE!"

Winston would then plunge deep while George hovered in the air, waiting for his friend...

…to come to the surface with a nice fish between his jaws.

Then they would go ashore, where they enjoyed many a delicious meal together.

George, however, had a very bad habit of playing pranks.

One day, while Winston was dozing with his neighbors, George flew over and yelled, "DANGER! DANGER!"

The crocodiles immediately plunged into the river, for crocodiles always believe warnings from crocodile birds.

They made a huge splash, which delighted George greatly.

When nothing happened, the crocodiles swam ashore and demanded, "Just what danger did you see?"

"I…I thought I saw a danger prowling through the jungle," George stammered. "A dangerous danger, a very scary dangerous danger."

The crocodiles grumbled that he wasn't telling the truth.

And the oldest and meanest snapped his jaws with a great clattering of teeth and warned, "A crocodile bird that plays pranks deserves to be eaten up!"

One afternoon, when the jungle was so steamy and hot that Winston had to take his nap in the water, George once again couldn't resist a prank and pushed his friend straight out into the middle of the river.

Winston woke up three miles downstream. When he finally got home after swimming all night against the current, the other crocodiles laughed and said, "This will teach you to be patient! Why don't you just eat up that bird as we told you to do?"

The thought of fishing alone out on the river without George made Winston too sad to even answer.

Then one early morning while they were out fishing, George looked down from Winston's snout and spotted a shoal of soft mud on the bottom of the river. Once again he couldn't resist a prank.

"DIVE! DIVE!" George shouted.

Down Winston dove, but instead of a fish he found his snout stuck firmly in the mud.

It was very funny at first to see a crocodile's feet and tail kicking and wagging in the air. But when George realized that his friend was stuck, he grew frightened.

He flew around and around, first to the hippopotamuses and then to the crocodiles, but no one offered to pull his friend from the mud. Instead they laughed and said this was what he deserved for all his pranks.

George flew back to his struggling friend. He tickled him, hoping that would help him to wiggle free, but Winston had lost all his patience and being tickled only made him angrier.

Then, suddenly, his legs stopped kicking and his tail stopped wagging and began to droop and droop and droop.

Soon the crocodiles and hippos swam over to see what the commotion was all about.

"We'll pull your friend out, but only if you promise to stand inside his jaws and be gobbled up, as you deserve."

"I don't care if he gobbles me up!" George pleaded. "Please, please, please save him!"

"Very well," they said, and the crocodiles and the hippos made a long chain and began to pull. They tugged and tugged until...

…with one final yank, Winston flew over their heads and landed on a far shore.

They all crowded about. As soon as Winston had recovered, one of the crocodiles said, "Now that we've pulled you out of the mud and saved your life, aren't you going to gobble up that bird of yours?"

Winston blew mud from his nostrils, and answered, "Why of course I'm going to gobble him up!" And this pleased them all very much.

Winston opened his huge jaws while the others urged George on, "Go on in as you promised! Climb in! Don't keep him waiting!"

Reluctantly, George stepped over Winston's sharp teeth and stood inside, waiting for his end to come.

Winston snapped his jaws shut. He then made a swallowing sound from deep down in his throat and stomach, followed by a loud burp. Once again, this pleased them all very much.

Then, when the last crocodile and the last hippopotamus had waddled back to the river ...

…Winston opened his jaws, and there was George, alive as ever, safe on his friend's soft tongue.

George stepped from Winston's mouth and thanked him again and again.

And from that day on, George didn't play any more pranks on his patient crocodile, although he was tempted to many, many times.

Crocodiles and Crocodile Birds

Real crocodile birds live in Africa and are about the size of pigeons but have long legs for wading. They are water birds, members of the plover family, and keep company with crocodiles along river banks. They are said to enter the open jaws of crocodiles to pick their teeth, but no scientist has ever reported seeing this. Instead, they have been found to pick leeches and lice from the crocodile's leathery, scaly skin. Crocodiles also like crocodile birds because they are constantly alert and cry out as soon as they see danger.

Many birds, even in our back yards, flutter about and warn other animals of danger. But between this small, smart bird and the giant, fierce crocodile there is a special friendship.

Real crocodiles are neither good nor bad. They are beautiful and scary, the same way a lion is beautiful and scary. They don't eat crocodile birds because nature gave them jaws to eat much larger animals. Crocodiles are reptiles and look much like their ancestors did back when other reptiles, the huge dinosaurs, roamed the earth.

Giuliano Cucco, illustrator, 1960s, Rome.

How This Book Came to Be

Fifty years ago in Rome, my friend Giuliano Cucco and I collaborated on four children's books, which I wrote and Giuliano illustrated. I brought Giuliano's artwork and my manuscripts back to New York City, hoping to find an editor who would publish our books. The art directors with whom I met were complimentary, but still I was told that reproducing the full-color illustrations would be too costly. At that time, in the early 1960s, most picture books still alternated between color and black-and-white illustrations. As Giuliano was in Rome and I was in New York, there was nothing for it but to put the work to the side.

Still, I held on to our work, carrying it from apartment to apartment and finally, no longer aware of what I had, to my attic in Sullivan County. Having completely forgotten about the work and nearly 50 years after it was created, I stumbled upon Giuliano's illustrations, bundled up in a portfolio, while laying down insulation in my attic.

To my surprise, the illustrations remained in perfect condition, as if the mice and squirrels that lived in my attic respected Giuliano's wonderful artistry. The stories, too, held up, and Claudia Bedrick of Enchanted Lion Books agreed to publish the books, with *Winston & George* being the first in the series.

Having lost contact with Giuliano, I set about sending letters to every Cucco in Italy. Just as I was about to give up, Giuliano's sister-in-law responded, and I learned that Giuliano and his wife had died in 2006.

We are dedicating this book to the memory of Giuliano Cucco and to Giona and Clara, the grandchildren he never knew.

— John Miller